MOTHER GOOSE

NURSERY RHYMES

A LITTLE APPLE CLASSIC
Illustrated by Gina Baek

KENNEBUNKPORT, MAINE

More Mother Goose Nursery Rhymes: A Little Apple Classic

13-Digit ISBN: 978-1-60433-951-2
10-Digit ISBN: 1-60433-951-9

This book may be ordered by mail from the publisher.
Please include $5.95 for postage and handling.
Please support your local bookseller first!

Books published by Cider Mill Press Book Publishers are available at special discounts for
bulk purchases in the United States by corporations, institutions, and other organizations.
For more information, please contact the publisher.

Applesauce Press is an imprint of
Cider Mill Press Book Publishers
"Where Good Books Are Ready for Press"
PO Box 454
12 Spring Street
Kennebunkport, Maine 04046

Visit us online at:
www.cidermillpress.com

Typography: Adobe Caslon and ITC Caslon
Printed in China

1 2 3 4 5 6 7 8 9 0
First Edition

BAA, BAA, BLACK SHEEP

Baa, baa, black sheep,
Have you any wool?
Yes, sir, yes, sir,
Three bags full:
One for the master,
One for the dame,
And one for the little boy
Who lives down the lane.

WHERE HAS MY LITTLE DOG GONE

Oh where, oh where
has my little dog gone?
Oh where, oh where
can he be?
With his ears cut short,
and his tail cut long,
Oh where, oh where
can he be?

RUB-A-
DUB-DUB

Rub-a-dub-dub,
Three men in a tub,
And who do you
think they be?
The butcher, the baker,
the candlestick maker,
And all of them out to sea.

COCK-A-DOODLE-DO!

Cock-a-doodle-do!
My dame has lost her shoe,
My master's lost his fiddle stick
And knows not what to do.
Cock-a-doodle-do!
What is my dame to do?
Till master finds his fiddle stick,
She'll dance without her shoe.

RING AROUND
THE ROSIE

Ring around the rosie,
A pocket full of posies,
Ashes! Ashes!
We all fall down.

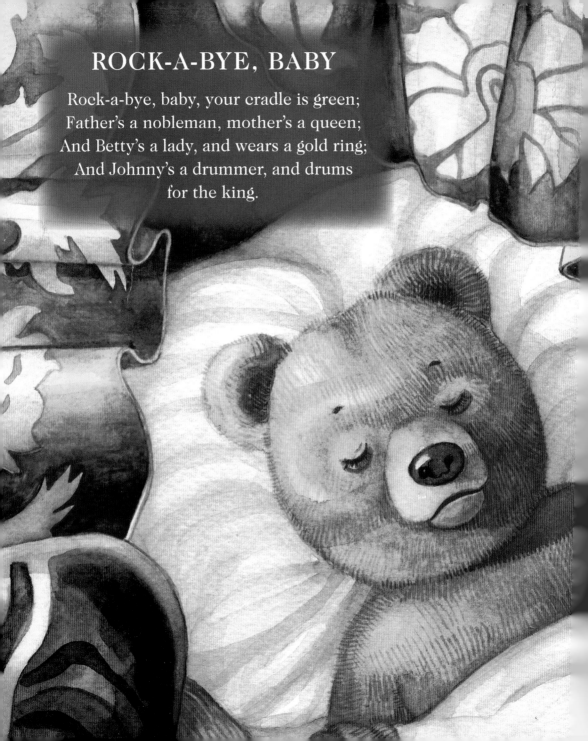

ROCK-A-BYE, BABY

Rock-a-bye, baby, your cradle is green;
Father's a nobleman, mother's a queen;
And Betty's a lady, and wears a gold ring;
And Johnny's a drummer, and drums
for the king.

PUSSY-CAT
AND QUEEN

"Pussy-cat, pussy-cat,
Where have you been?"
"I've been to London
To look at the Queen."
"Pussy-cat, pussy-cat,
What did you there?"
"I frightened a little mouse
Under her chair."

LITTLE BO-PEEP

Little Bo-Peep has lost her sheep,
And can't tell where to find them;
Leave them alone, and they'll come home,
Bringing their tails behind them.

LITTLE MISS MUFFET

Little Miss Muffet
Sat on a tuffet,
Eating her curds and whey;
Along came a spider,
Who sat down beside her,
And frightened Miss Muffet away.

THERE WAS AN OLD WOMAN

There was an old woman who lived in a shoe.
She had so many children she didn't know what to do.
She gave them some broth without any bread;
And kissed them all sweetly and put them to bed.

ABOUT APPLESAUCE PRESS

Good ideas ripen with time. From seed to harvest, Applesauce Press crafts books with beautiful designs, creative formats, and kid-friendly information on a variety of fascinating topics. Like our parent company, Cider Mill Press Book Publishers, our press bears fruit twice a year, publishing a new crop of titles each spring and fall.

Write to us at:
PO Box 454
Kennebunkport, ME 04046

Or visit us online at:
www.cidermillpress.com